MW01527016

INTO THE RED SEA

Tales from a Cold War Sailor

Ross A. Webber

Lieutenant, USNR (ret)
Professor of Management Emeritus
The Wharton School, University of Pennsylvania

Copyright 2011 Ross A. Webber

All rights reserved

ISBN-13: 978-1460920954

ISBN-10: 1460920953

TO:

Wells McCaffrey Webber

The last, but not the least

and

Genevieve Lobner

The first of many

Preface

Although now a bit pock marked from the September 11, 2001 terrorist attack on the World Trade Center, the Federal Office Building at 90 Church Street in Manhattan is an iconic site where hundreds of thousands of young men and women volunteers and draftees have been inducted into the Armed Services of the United States of America. For me it was on my 18th birthday in 1952 when I was sworn into the United States Navy in the offices of the Commandant of the Third Naval District. It was especially exciting because I was just old enough to remember sitting in a movie theater in the early 1940's watching a Pathe' News feature of young draftees being sworn in to confront the Nazi and Japanese challenges.

My parents had driven me into the city from our suburban home in New Rochelle. I was a bit in awe (and perhaps envious) of the young men around me who appeared to be handling the big day on their own. I had been awarded a coveted Naval Reserve Officers Training Corps (NROTC) scholarship that would pay my full college tuition in return for a commitment of one day a week during the school year, three eight week summer deployments, active duty for three years, plus seven years in the ready reserve. So I was no longer subject to the draft and not heading immediately to the Korean War then in progress. Nonetheless, we were warned that if we didn't maintain our college grades we would be quickly called to active duty as enlisted seamen.

After our swearing in, I received a physical examination and numerous inoculations for unheard of diseases – an experience to be repeated too many times while sailing around the world. Of particular concern that day was my body weight: one hundred twenty four pounds was the minimum allowed for my five foot, eight inch height. Stuffing myself with Milky Ways, I cleared the hurdle by three pounds.

A month later I found myself as a midshipman on an extremely hot Princeton University soccer field learning how to take orders from a Marine drill instructor who didn't seem to realize that I expected to be trained as a future Admiral Nimitz rather than a Marine rifleman.

Over the following seven years I was blessed with an incredible experience filled with challenge, fatigue, exhilaration, failure, and success – certainly the greatest learning experience of my life. I served on a battleship and two destroyers, along with short rides on a submarine, troop transport, aircraft carrier and a Canadian frigate; sailed on five of the seven seas and visited twenty-six countries. The following stories describe some of the exciting, discouraging, satisfying, frustrating, serious, tragic and humorous events experienced in these assignments. I hope some readers will remember fondly their own naval experiences.

Events are described as I best remember them, but of course, I can't swear to their total accuracy. Fortunately, my girlfriend, future wife and still present spouse kept every one of the hundreds of letters which I wrote her over the seven years covered in these stories so I have a contemporaneous check on my recollections. Most of the photographs included were taken over fifty years ago with my small Voigtlander so the quality is not the best. But they are authentic. Illustrations from U.S. Government sources are noted. I am especially grateful to the superior officers under whom I served, especially Commanders Joseph A. Bachhuber, USN and William W. Schweer, USN who were my Commanding Officers on the USS Cotten (DD669). Their commitment to the protection of the United States of America deserves our gratitude. I remember fondly those other junior officers who were so helpful in my learning how to be a naval officer: Dick Emmett, Bruce Hilyard, John Fenlon, Sam Koutas, John Lee, Tom Murray, Dick Myers, and Wally Norton.

I am grateful to Jim Henderson, John Buzby and Lee (and his wife Lynn) McMillion, fellow Navy veterans, for their helpful editorial comments and encouragement. Judith Webber provided invaluable assistance with the book's design. Special thanks go to my wife Mary Louise for her thoughtfulness in keeping my long ago letters letters and for correcting many errors, but I am even more thankful for her staunch support during my active duty service. The Commodore of Destroyer Squadron Thirty thought she was the "perfect Navy wife" because of her poise, confidence and self-reliance. When at sea I thought about her constantly, but she was never a worry.

Ross A. Webber

Table of Contents

1. BOARDING THE IOWA

I survived my freshman year without a failure that would have sent me to Korea so on July 10, 1953 I took my first solo long distance train ride from New York's Penn Station to Norfolk, Virginia.   Saying goodbye to my parents late in the evening seemed like the end of my childhood. And so it was because except for short visits, I never lived at my parent's home again.

Arriving at the U.S. Naval Base and boarding the U.S.S. Iowa (BB-61) at 0500 (5:00AM) was like descending into Dante's inferno. It was so hot and noisy. Built long before the introduction of shipboard air cooling, the Iowa was a World War II vessel whose only antidote for the incredible July below decks heat was the incessant sound from the giant blowers bringing stifling Tidewater humidity into the 45,000 ton ship's bowels.

I was conducted to the large bunk filled compartment that was to be my home for the next two months. As

Author as Midshipman 1952

I had arrived early, I was given a choice of which of the three high bunks I preferred. By blind luck I choose the top rack giving me just eighteen inches below the overhead (ceiling), but no sagging bottom above me would ever be a nuisance. And I came to feel almost comfy in my tiny space. Being on top, however, made it more difficult when we were ordered to "air bedding" by dragging our mattresses topside to lay them on the ship's life lines.

Reveille was at 0600 with the usual loudspeaker command of "Reveille, reveille; rise and shine; heave out and trice up; clean sweep down fore and aft; the smoking lamp is lighted in all authorized spaces." The heaving out and tricing up were a throwback to sailing ship days when sailors slept in hammocks. Sometimes, a playful Boatswain's Mate would alter the announcement to "Wakee, Wakee; rise and shine; the cooks are in the galley and the beans are on the line." And on Sundays we could wait in line outside on the main deck and receive fresh cooked eggs at the galley hatch. Warm nights could find us sitting on the fantail near the ship's stern watching a movie projected onto a screen suspended from the seaplane crane.

13

Being early became a critical element in maintaining my sense of control and individuality. I trained myself to wake up thirty minutes before reveille so I could get to the head (bathroom) to wash and shave before the mass of my new shipmates. For our first Saturday Captain's inspection (which fell on my 19th birthday), I gave particular attention to my shaving only to find while standing at attention that blood was running down my chin and falling on my white uniform. I did have beautifully spit-shined shoes however. Even the gold braided Captain smiled at that as he asked my name.

Especially appreciated about arising early was not having to sit cheek to cheek on the public trough that served as the toilet – thus evading the thankfully rare occasions then some jokester would float a lighted chunk of paper that would pass below the several exposed tender bottoms.

Like much military life, there is always an element of "hurry up and wait." One had to be ready at a precise time, but all conditions to proceed might not be in place. So, in this pre-IPOD, pre-Walkman, pre-Blackberry era, we learned to always carry a paperback book at the ready. On one particularly overcast day of heavy seas, I was feeling miserable while deep into Nicholas Monsarrat's novel *The Cruel Sea* with its depiction of the World War Two travail of the Royal Navy Corvette HMS Compass Rose being tossed about like a leaf on the North Atlantic. I was fortunate to be on a more stable vessel, but the sea was the same and most of us were quite seasick and wanted to resign. I could emphasize with that buffeted British crew.

If my own sleeping compartment was hot, my first watch station was even worse. My assignment was to maintain the water level in the number two engine condensate pump. I had to watch the level in a glass tube, opening and closing a water intake valve as needed – a boring job, but one of high importance in a manually operated warship. Letting the water level get too low or high could disable a main boiler and steam turbine engine, virtually stopping the ship. The heat and noise generated by the boilers and reduction gear was beyond belief. But one learned to acclimate and stay awake.

Years later when I become an officer, I was assigned to serve as a judge for the court marshal of a nineteen year seaman who had fallen asleep while manning the same valve on another ship. The chief of his watch had tied the sleepy sailor's shoe laces to the deck grating before yelling at him to wake up. The unfortunate young man jumped and fell on his face. Remembering my own experience at the boring job, I felt some sympathy for his plight.

Luckily for me, my second watch station training was in a happier location – way up in the superstructure on the eleventh level above the first (main) deck. I was the forward port lookout perched on an open platform just above the ship's command bridge. With my (heavy) binoculars I would scan the horizon in ten degree increments earnestly looking for something threatening or at least interesting enough to report to the bridge. Visions of spotting a half hidden rocky shoal or a submarine's periscope wake danced in my head.

As a member of the Operations Division I also spent some time at the ship's wheel as the helmsman. The wheel was still large and turned real cables that controlled the rudder (unlike today's ships with tiny computer connected wheels). It was a thrilling assignment until I realized how limited was my vision. To protect the helm from enemy fire, I was surrounded by reinforced sixteen inch armor that provided only small slits to see outside. Everyone on the open bridge could be killed, but the helmsman could continue the course last assigned, but it would have been difficult to maneuver the ship on his own.

In the years after World War Two, U.S. Navy ships underwent repeated modifications, especially in electronics, communications and radar. Many of these changes were located on the massive superstructure on the Iowa. The new electronics took up less space than the electro-mechanical systems they had replaced. As a result, the Operations Division found itself with an empty 10 x 15 feet space on the 011 level (that's 11 stories up). With the creativity common to American sailors, they had made up a sign labeling the compartment "paint locker." No paint was ever stored there however. Rather it was outfitted with cots to meet the sailor's most urgent need at sea: sleep. At any given time, three to five sailors would be sacked out.

One Saturday during Captain's Inspection, I was assigned to stand by the disguised compartment. During an inspection all rooms are expected to be open. But no one had told me and I had no key.

17

Asked what the compartment was for, I naively echoed the sign. However, the Captain knew his ship. He said there was no authorized paint locker for the Operations Division. I was directed to find the key and open the space. The cots were revealed (luckily, no one was then sleeping in them). So ended the secret Operations Division hideaway.

My general quarters (battle) station was as far from the 011 deck as one could get to in the bowels of the Iowa's hull three decks below the 001 main deck. I was the lower right powder hoist operator in the second of three sixteen inch gun turrets. The powder was stored in a magazine deep below the ship's it waterline behind the hull's sixteen inch armor plate to protect it from enemy shells. I loaded six sixty pound silk encased bags of powder into the hoist for each firing of the gun which could send a 2000 pound shell up to fifteen miles. I was so far below the ship's waterline that the sound of the guns firing produced only a muffled roar and shuttering of the hull.

USS Iowa firing a full broadside (US Navy photograph)

Many years later on April 19, 1989, my successors were very unlucky when a powder explosion killed forty seven sailors in the Iowa's number two turret.

Just before entering the Firth of Forth for Edinburgh, Scotland on July 26, 1953 the Iowa's Captain announced the signing of the Korean War Armistice. What followed was an extremely happy five liberty days for the crew who for years afterward raved about the kindness of the Scots and receptivity of the young women (rumor said that twelve US sailors were married during our visit). On July 27, I wrote to my girlfriend, "The girls just proposition me right on the street!" Of course, I wanted to reassure her that I was not succumbing.

In Scotland we had very few cases of drunkenness. Unhappily, in our second port, Oslo, Norway the girls were much more reserved so our crew's behavior ashore became more of a problem.

2. A GENTLEMANLY MARINE

A portion of a Midshipman's training is devoted to the Marine Corps. Mine was at the Naval Amphibious Training Base in Little Creek, Virginia – a world class area for a high heat-humidity index. The only respite from the July 1954 heat was in the base auditorium where we were compelled to watch a film of male penises rotting away from venereal disease (I walked out claiming this was not relevant to me; I was severely chastised by the base chaplain). More positively, we also were shown the stirring images and music from Richard Rodgers' "Victory at Sea." To ensure that we were not sleeping, a drill instructor would patrol the isles with his swagger stick at the ready to "tap" a napping head. A touch and one snapped to attention.

My Platoon Sergeant M, thankfully, was not a tapper. He was also not your TV stereotyped Gomer Pyle or crew cut martinet. No, he was a consummate gentleman. A Navy Cross winner and former Marine Corps Enlisted Man of the Year from whom I never heard a swear word. He made sure the Catholics in his group attended Mass on Sundays accompanying them in a uniform with trousers creased as sharply as his sword. He had been carefully selected to appeal to what was thought to be an elite group of Princeton Midshipmen. He of course introduced us to the typical leatherneck duties: peeling spuds, keeping socks clean, assembling our weapons in the dark, and husbanding our water. Having been taught on maneuvers to conserve water strictly, it is difficult to identify with bottle carrying young people today who feel they must maximize hydration.

The main objective of our training was participating in an amphibious landing. We boarded the 10,000 ton troop ship USS Latimer (APA-152) for a mercifully short three days. I was introduced to the joys of a five high rack of bunks in a 250 person compartment where you tried to avoid being berthed under an overweight colleague – especially since we had no lockers and all gear was stored on your bunk. I learned to escape by sleeping in a 40 mm gun tub. We all learned to climb down a rope mesh into a small Higgins landing craft (LCMs and LCVPs) The descent was not especially difficult except that we carried a fifty pound pack on our backs and the landing craft was rising and falling ten feet or so in the rolling sea. One's feet could hit the deck too soon or too late.

Sprained and broken ankles were not uncommon. The ride toward the Camp Pendleton beach was thrilling with the pounding of the flat bottomed hull and spray breaking over the bow door from a fifty knot wind. We were swamped from a wave breaking over our port side as we turned. Luckily, no live bullets were being fired at us.

USS Latimer APA-152 (US Navy photograph)

The purpose of the flat hull was to allow the craft to run up on a sandy beach as far as possible allowing thirty six Marines to debark on near dry land. Alas, most landings are not made on sandy beaches in Virginia or South Carolina. Hitting sand bars, hidden rocks and underwater obstacles could result in the soldiers finding themselves in deep water weighted down by their equipment. Numerous troops drowned in the June 1944 Normandy landings. In our training landings ten years later we only got wet. But even that triviality created a real struggle to wade through soggy mud and sand with full battle pack. I certainly wished that I was a lot bigger and stronger.

Sergeant M. had bright white hair and he looked ancient to me (I now realize he could have been only fifty years old). Yet he waded ashore alongside us as if he had buoyant legs. It was certainly easier for him than were his World War Two Pacific landings. What was buoyant of course was his spirit. He taught me that the toughest of men could be a gentleman serving as a model for high standards.

To the bemusement or consternation of my watch members years later when I was the Officer of the Deck on our ship, I forbid the use of the ubiquitous

"F...ing" word that seemed mandatory several times in every sentence. Also banned were the less wholesome euphemisms for female anatomy. My enlisted colleagues would struggle with expressing themselves but in time took it good naturedly (I wonder if in today's litigious climate whether I would be sued for violating a person's right to freedom of speech, but then today Goldman Sachs is trying to clean up its E-mails). Foul language reflects semantic laziness; resorting to the base when finding accurate

Hitting the Beach from an LCVP

words is too difficult. When I was ending my tour on board, a senior First Class Boatswain's Mate even thanked me for setting such a high tone on the bridge. Others probably thought I was just a prude.

Perhaps I was. The conclusion of our Norfolk training included a dance with assorted daughters of senior naval officers and local gentry. The after dance party shattered my image of southern gentility. Never had I seen girls drink so much so fast. I was not adverse to consuming alcohol, but not at their rate. After not getting a response to her fairly obvious sexual invitation), one girl gave me the ultimate put down: "You sure don't behave like other Princeton men!" Perhaps, I was just afraid that one complaint to her "Commandant of the Marine Corps" grandfather would mean the abrupt end to my fledging naval career.

That young woman might have been on to something. My Princeton NROTC unit was ranked 26 of 26 units that summer. We thought it was prejudice, but the powers that be saw a lack of seriousness and excessive drinking (after all, the Dartmouth contingent was ranked 25th and that should say something).

Today when walking on the university campus where I teach, I can hear angelic looking female students carelessly use language as bad as my seamen so many years ago. And I wonder what it means.

Into the Red Sea

3. "THE RIVETS ARE POPPING OUT!"

The SNJ (T-6 Texan in US Air Force terminology) was a pre World War II low mono-winged trainer for aviation cadets. It had a huge wing surface that generated great lift even with an underpowered engine. It could fly slowly at less than one hundred knots and was easy to maneuver - hence the SNJ's use as a primary trainer. Most of my fellow twenty year old Navy Midshipmen had never before been in a small plane. Indeed, in the early 1950's, the majority had never flown in any kind of aircraft before being conveyed to Corpus Christi, Texas, for training.

We were flown from Norfolk to Corpus Christi on July 14, 1954 in Navy four-engine DC 4's. This was a big upgrade from the old warhorse two engine DC 3's (The Dakota of WWII fame) because in 1953 one had crashed killing all forty midshipman aboard.

My instructor was a veteran flying Chief Petty Officer, one of less than 150 enlisted naval aviators then still

Into the Red Sea

SNJ (Texans) in flight (US Navy photograph)

in service. He had a deeply lined Marlborough Man Texas face that obviously had spent a lot of time in the air and sun. And you could do that in an SNJ because it had an all glass canopy that provided 180 degrees of visibility and could be pushed back for *al fresco* flying. He even had a white silk scarf tied around his neck for a Baron von Richtofen-Peanuts look. He sat in the front seat with me behind with duplicate controls.

On our first flight as we were doing a tight turn I looked over the starboard wing and was alarmed to see rivets popping out. I yelled my alarm on the intercom. Laconically he responded that, "they are always falling out of this old bird." Luckily, there was enough redundancy that the wings didn't fall off.

I loved those SNJ flights. By July 16, I wanted passionately to be a Navy pilot. Alas, my romance with naval flight ended quickly when we graduated to a jet trainer, the T-O2 (T-33 Shooting Star in the Air Force). The change was dramatic. The action pace was so much faster and I had to wear a hard helmet that covered my whole head with a glass visor. Even worse, the jet's canopy was a hydraulically controlled solid Plexiglas that couldn't be opened in flight - unless you activated the ejection seat! Even though I could see for a hundred miles, I felt claustrophobic in a way I had never felt at sea - confined, diminished, part of the machinery rather than in control. I preferred the salt spray in my face so I elected to go to sea.

Into the Red Sea

Lockeed T-O2 (T-33 Shooting Star. US Air Force photograph)

To top off my Naval Air experience, I was put on report for putting my bunk cover on upset down. For this dangerous transgression, I received five demerits and one hour extra duty standing guard in the hot sun. I concluded that flying entailed too much "chickenshit."

In subsequent years serving on destroyers I got plenty of ocean spray — and virtually no fowl excrement.

4: PARTYING IN SCANDINAVIA

I boarded my first destroyer for summer training on July 10, 1955. It was the last sea opportunity to prepare us Midshipman for our soon to come commissioned officer status. She was the USS Moale (DD-693), a Sumner 2100 ton class. I reported in Norfolk, Virginia, and was immediately impressed with how small the ship was in comparison with the Iowa. It moved up and down while just sitting at the dock! In the days of big military and budgets and cold war flag showing, we were to accompany the battleship USS Wisconsin (BB-64) to a number of delightful ports including Bergen, Norway and Stockholm, Sweden.

When we put to sea I quickly learned what smaller meant – seasickness. It was my first experience with the overwhelming physical and psychological symptoms: headache, nausea, vomiting and hopeless feelings. First, you are afraid that you might die; then you're afraid that you won't.

Thankfully, time and acclimation healed all ills and I grew to love the intimacy and informality of the

Moale along with sense of being alive when bounding through a choppy sea. This sense of adventure was enriched by my first opportunity to stand watch on the bridge as junior officer of the deck. Bracing myself to the roll of the vessel and feeling the salt spray mist on my face conjured up images of C.S. Forester's Horatio Hornblower enforcing the blockade off of Brest at the height of the Napoleonic era. I knew that the bridge was where I wanted to be. It was a great thrill to be given the conn as we

USS Moale (DD-693. US Navy photograph)

accompanied the Wisconsin through the treacherous waters of the Kattegut strait between Jutland and Sweden.

The Moale's bridge provided my first exposure to a central feature of naval life — rehearsing responses to various emergencies. At least once a four hour watch, the officer in charge would report a nonexistent sonar echo or unidentified radar blip

USS Wisconsin (BB-64)

precipitating a planned sequence of responses. Similarly, he would surreptitiously disconnect the steering cable so the helmsman no longer had control of the rudder. The helmsman would feel the looseness in his wheel and yell out "Lost rudder control." Then the officer of the deck would call After Steering to see if they had detected the change and taken control.

After Steering was located in the ship's stern well away from the bridge so that they might survive if the bridge were damaged. The isolated location, however, made it all too easy for its crew to play cards or fall asleep. This drill was primarily to keep them alert, but all these rehearsals were intended to make routine the correct responses to unexpected but anticipated emergencies. Many years later when I was heavily involved in business organizations, I was disturbed by how little time was invested in anticipating and rehearsing for the unexpected (all too evident in the financial debacle of the recent past).

As a third year midshipman, I had quite a lot of paperwork assignments that required sitting below decks at a desk in a gyrating compartment. Along with engineering, gunnery, and navigation, I was designated as the ship's recreation officer. It was a much bigger assignment that it sounds. The Captain asked for the names and addresses of all the midshipmen's parents; the Chaplain asked me to recruit ten men for his choir; I was also directed to arrange for dances in Bergin and Stockholm. The respective United States Consul and Ambassador were to arrange for the females while I was to supply twenty six males. This entailed getting commitments to attend as well as agreements to a code of conduct. This would have been easier if my guys had known how beautiful the girls would be. Two of them took a friend and me to visit the composer Edvard Grieg's home memorialized in his "Wedding Day at Troldhaugen." His music has been a favorite ever since. All in all, the US Foreign Service did a better job than I did. But, I got a lot of the credit.

After departing Bergin we sailed through the English Channel and then southwest enroute to Guantanamo Bay, Cuba (GITMO is Navy parlance) on the longest leg of the cruise. A few days later, I was surprised by an invitation to breakfast with the Captain. He was one of the most magnetic men I ever met and he easily persuaded me (without even issuing an order) to organize a "happy hour talent show" to break up the sixteen day cruise tedium. Of course, this was to be a happy hour without alcohol so the chief activity was to be a series of acts that I was to organize. I soon found myself sitting in the fo'c'sle auditioning two harmonica players. On August 13, I wrote Mary Lou that, "It will be a miracle if it works."

Well, no miracle occurred on the North Atlantic that summer, but the day's entertainment was delivered with much enthusiasm and received gratefully. Sailors can have fun without beer.

5. AVOIDING ENGINEERING

A week after my college graduation, on June 24, 1956 I reported on board the USS Cotten (DD-669) in the Philadelphia Naval Shipyard. She was a 1940's built Fletcher class Destroyer, 376 feet long displacing 2050 tons with a crew of 329. I was greeted by a grizzled old Executive Officer (second in command) who was a very senior Lieutenant (probably all of thirty five years old!). He was in his cabin playing poker with my new officer colleagues when I appeared. After the game he talked to me about my future assignments.

When the XO saw that I had majored in mechanical engineering he told me he would appoint me an Assistant Division Officer in the Engineering Department. Remembering the overheated engineering spaces on the Iowa, I was anxious to avoid that assignment. Deferentially, I asked him who else would be reporting. He said that a new engineering graduate from Purdue University would

The author as a new Ensign June 1956

also be coming aboard. Swallowing my Princeton pride, I quickly suggested that Purdue had a much stronger engineering program and that I would be of more value to the ship as a deck officer. Richard Myers, the new Ensign from Purdue, became an exceedingly competent Chief Engineer and an exemplary officer.

I got my deck preference and spent the following three years at sea in gunnery and operations where I served as Officer of the Deck (OOD) conning my ship in high speed plane guard screening with some huge fleet aircraft carriers including the USS Franklin D. Roosevelt (CVA-42) and the USS Saratoga (CVA 60). The sun, the salt spray, the signal flags fluttering in the wind all appealed to my romantic Lord Nelson side, providing some of life's peak experiences.

Before any peak experience, however, I was handed a bill of $20 for a month's board and a $16 mess assessment. I had no idea that I had to pay for my own food and lodging on board the ship out of my $222 monthly pay. Unfortunately, I was $800 in debt and had not yet been paid! Luckily, on June 25 I was sent with a travel allowance to Torpedo School in Newport Rhode Island where I experienced life in the

USS Cotten DD-669

Base Officers' Quarters (BOQ – sometimes referred to as "Bachelor's" OQ). It was sort of like college, but duller - with miles of linoleum covered floors and no women.

In my early assignment as torpedo officer on the Cotten, my General Quarters station was on the torpedo director platform just behind the after ship's funnel. Perched just above the ten 21 inch torpedo tubes, the exhaust from the ship's four oil burning boilers would stream directly through my platform. The most noxious component of the smoke was sulfur dioxide to which I developed a chronic sensitivity. Walking behind a diesel burning truck today can instantly transport me back to that odious platform.

On a more positive note, the psychologist Abraham Maslow described peak experiences as the quintessential blend of intellect and emotion, analysis and instinct – situations in which one transcends oneself. A clear manifestation for me was when I had graduated to the bridge conning the ship during a live torpedo firing exercise in the Caribbean off of Cuba. At high speed I was to maneuver our destroyer and fire a torpedo at a moving target. For some reason the plotting crew in the Combat Information Center (CIC) below was experiencing difficulties in solving the trigonometric problem. Somehow the whole diagram was clear in my mind and I maneuvered the ship perfectly (at least in the opinion of the exercise inspector). Torpedo School had prepared me to visualize the solution.

In retrospect I remember the thirty minutes as more instinctual than rational. Luck is certainly more likely to come to the prepared mind. I received a letter of commendation for the events of that sun splashed day. We reached the GITMO Naval Base Officers'

Club Bar just fifteen minutes before its closing. The Captain had already ordered three rounds of Anjeho Punch for all of us. They tasted so good.

Torpedo firing

6. DON'T GET MARRIED!

When I reported to the Cotten, the Executive Officer strongly urged me not to get married. Explaining how the ship was to deploy for training in the Caribbean followed by a January departure to foreign waters, he argued that the combined stress of the Navy and a new marriage would be burdensome. I later discovered what a playboy the XO was, so perhaps he had really been warning me about how much "fun" he thought I would miss in the various exotic ports we would be visiting (or if I didn't miss the fun, how guilty I would feel).

I nodded my head but thought that there was no way my fiancé and I would change our December wedding plan. However a providential alternative soon presented itself. The ship needed an Assistant Anti-submarine Warfare Officer so I was given the tough assignment of attending the eight week ASW course at The Fleet Sonar School in Key West, Florida. Having a chance to spend the fall in Key West, we moved up our wedding date to September, a week before my school reporting date.

There was a complication however. I and the ship would be training in Guantanamo, Cuba, until two days before the rescheduled wedding date. My future wife and her mother would have to make all the plans on their own (something I didn't really miss). But the timing almost torpedoed the wedding.

Upon my returning from Cuba, we discovered that there weren't enough days between getting the marriage license and receiving the required blood test results. In panic, my future mother-in-law called a city judge friend who was able to cut the red tape. The wedding came off as planned and the Cotten's Commanding Officer even attended.

Anti-submarine Warfare School was challenging and enjoyable. And it fit my intellectual skills - turning out to be the only school I ever attended where I graduated first in my class. I got to ride in an old WWII diesel submarine and get a taste of the tension when you are under water awaiting the sound of a dummy hedgehog rocket or Mark 32 antisubmarine

USS Cotten Commanding Officer at author's wedding
September 29, 1956

torpedo tapping the hull to signal that in a real war you would be dead.

When I returned to the ship from Key West, Captain Bachhuber expressed his pleasure with my performance, but also observed that I was the first groom that he had ever seen who had returned from his honeymoon pregnant. My new wife was such a good cook and I so enjoyed the chocolate hot fudge marshmallow sundaes that she made that I had gained twenty pounds in eight weeks.

Luckily, Navy food while I was at sea for the next five months returned me to normal weight. My new bride, however, put some of my lost inches onto her waist. When I returned, she was five months pregnant.

7. I KILL A COW

Certain Caribbean islands off of Puerto Rico have been pounded endlessly by United States Navy warships and aircraft. Because the weather usually is so lovely, Vieques and Culebra especially were used for target practice. Civilian inhabitants of the islands often complained about missed targets, wayward shots and unexploded ordnance. Thankfully, they are no longer being fired upon. Back when I was directing gunfire at these picturesque isles, however, the inhabitants were less complaining – or were ignored.

My first shore bombardment was as the ship's fire control officer. I was stationed down in the ship's bowels manning a Ford made mechanical computer. About the size of a steamer trunk, it was an analog wonder full of intermeshed gears which gave off an impressive whirring sound. The gear ratios could be altered manually for air and powder temperatures, wind direction and speed, and of course target elevation and distance. All were ground together by the machinery to control the elevation of our main battery of five inch, thirty eight caliber guns. Our shells were tiny compared with the sixteen inch projectiles on a battleship, but we could maneuver much closer to the targets for shore bombardment. So that is what we did off of Culebra Island. My First Class Fire Controlman entered all the necessary numbers. We fired our first salvo. It landed in farmer's field more than a mile off target. No one on board even saw it land, but we heard about the poor cow.

The Captain was not pleased. On August 7, 1956 I wrote to Mary Lou with the understatement, "The Captain was quite angry." He demanded to know what went wrong. I replied in the manner that I had been taught as a Midshipman, "I don't know Sir, but I will find out."   And I did. Temperatures had been cranked in incorrectly, reversing the plus and minus signs. And I had not checked them. Doing its job loyally and blindly, the computer compensated by increasing the gun's elevation increasing the range. On this occasion I was certainly happy that I had not been given my other assignment as fire control officer – to go ashore and spot the shell landings correcting them on target. Not if I was firing at me.

Years later when electronic digital computers came along, I already knew the aphorism, "Garbage in, garbage out."

Into the Red Sea

8. A BIRTH AT SEA

My wife and I were living in Newport on the second floor of a former stable of a Bellevue Avenue mansion just up the road from the Vanderbilt's famous summer cottage, "The Breakers." Our first born child was due in mid August 1957. Since my ship was not due to depart Newport for the North Atlantic until September 3, it appeared likely that I would be around for the big event. But August ended without delivery so I left the ship in Newport to spend Labor Day weekend with my wife in New York where she was awaiting the stork. But I committed the greatest error of my Navy career: I left the ship with the only keys to the cryptographic room.

The cryptographic machine was a mysterious device with multiple electro-mechanical rotors that sorted numbers and letters in random ways. I can still smell the static electricity odor that permeated the tiny compartment in which I worked alone decoding secret messages.   Without the precious keys that were in my pocket in a taxi heading for the Providence train station, no one could access the

Into the Red Sea

machine if a high priority message was received. So wearily and in a fog of anxiety I had to return to the ship to deposit the keys before traveling on to my expectant wife.

This was long before the era of induced or scheduled deliveries. So we were committed to awaiting nature's course. Unfortunately, nature didn't produce so at midnight on September 2, I had to catch a train from Greenwich, Connecticut to meet my ship for its departure the next morning. Saying good bye to my nine plus months pregnant wife was tough – but an event not unknown to military personnel. But she was so pregnant I wasn't sure she could it make it home from the station.

I made it to Newport just before dawn to a deserted pier where I would await a tender to take me out to my moored ship. The pier appeared to be continuously moving. As the light brightened, I could see that the movement was actually a sea of wharf rats – the biggest that I had ever seen. It was their time of day, not mine. I feared that I would become rodent food before I became a father. Thankfully, with the dawn the rats dispersed back to their dens and I went out to the ship.

54

We put to sea as scheduled. It was the height of the Cold War so our squadron departed Narragansett Bay under radio silence. We could receive messages, but we could neither send nor acknowledge receipt. The birth announcement came four hours later. I was standing watch on the bridge heading east northeast under low clouds and a substantial sea when the Captain showed me the decoded message announcing the birth of Sarah Ruth Webber, weight eight pounds, thirteen ounces, Mother doing fine, etc. In those days we could still smoke on board so we lighted up a few cigars and celebrated my new fatherhood. I didn't see or talk to my wife until Sarah Ruth was three months old.

I often wondered if the Russians monitoring our radio traffic thought the birth announcement was code for some top secret new American weapon development.

Into the Red Sea

Signaling

9. THE EMPTY BOX

The most practical lesson I learned from my Navy life was neatness and organization. Appearance was important and to maintain a presentable uniform required expert packing and periodic repair. Virtually every item is rolled tightly to minimize wrinkles and maximize storage efficiency. And given that that one sometimes had to dress quickly in near darkness, having items in assigned places was critical. "Make and mend" days are a naval tradition.

The United States Navy has continued the practice of the Royal Navy that commissioned officers are responsible for purchasing their food and uniforms at their own expense. At the $222 per month that I earned as an Ensign, paying $75 for a dress blue suit was a real stretch. Aboard ship, the officers were organized into a Ward Room Mess that collectively was responsible for assessing the funds and purchasing the food. The Treasurer position was rotated among the junior members.

For a year I served as the treasurer working with our first class petty officer steward. I did the job without too many complaints – except for the time I bought langouste in San Juan. That precipitated a small outbreak of food poisoning. Luckily, it was only among those few who had eaten it on Saturday, the second day that it had been served. Never keep shellfish overnight.

Like a college fraternity, we had a continuing problem of officers raiding the Ward Room pantry refrigerator late at night. This often fouled up the chief steward's planned meals for the next day. After complaints and appeals had no effect, we resorted to the unpopular step of locking the refrigerator at night. How ironic that I had to do what my mother only had threatened to do when her six children were all at home.

Our Chief Steward was actually a very good cook who would often purchase food from the crew's mess and add a few wrinkles that would transfer it into a fine meal. In Karachi, Pakistan he learned to prepare curry which we came to enjoy. Months later, he taught my wife how to make curry dishes which have continued to be one of my favorite meals. On Sundays when I had the duty, my wife would come onboard for dinner and our baby daughter would nap in the

Captain's cabin while the duty officers would enjoy memories of Karachi.

Ship's equipment and spare parts were more important than officers' meals of course. I learned to be near paranoid in this area. One of my assignments was serving as the ship's Anti-Submarine Warfare Officer. This put me in charge of the sonar electronics so critical to fulfilling a destroyer's mission to detect and destroy enemy submarines.

When one assumes responsibility for a department (or a ship's command), one personally signs for the equipment and spare parts inventory associated with the unit. The departing officer will show you an inventoried (apparently) list. The pressure of time and a culture of trust can lead a naïve replacement to sign and move on. Beware!

We were in the Mediterranean screening a Sixth Fleet task force when our sonar failed. This had to be immediately reported to the fleet commander, but we assured him that we would repair our equipment in a few hours. Running down to the storage locker with my senior Sonar Petty Officer, we threw open the large box presumed to contain the key vacuum

59

tube. Alas, the box labeled "Cavitron" was empty. And there was no other replacement on board. We could only guess that some predecessors had forgotten to order a replacement or had declined to do so in order to meet a budget. More personally, I had neglected to verify the inventory when assuming responsibility. We had only looked at the box labels. With utter chagrin I had to inform the Captain that we would have no sonar until the missing part was `brought on board. And he had to report to the Admiral as well as the Bureau of Ships in Washington, DC that the USS Cotten would not be able to perform its duties.

This is the stuff that derails careers. We found a replacement on a sister squadron ship (which was not appreciated because it put them at risk), but I certainly learned the power of the old cliché, "never, never, never, never assume."

10. SWIMMING IN THE DEEP

When I was a first-year Midshipman on the Iowa, a fellow middy jumped overboard. At fifteen knots we were long gone before anyone realized he was missing. Fortunately, a trailing Destroyer saw him and he was recovered. I heard later that it was not without a struggle. Literature's greatest writers have written of the ocean's mystery, allure and inconstancy - often alluding to its feminine nature. James Cameron's film "The Abyss" is his scariest. The idea of being in an ocean with a thousand or more fathoms below is terrifying. And unlike most sailors, I am a fairly good swimmer.

Yet one day the Cotten's Captain proposed that we all go swimming. We were in the southern Atlantic Ocean making a long passage from Cape Town, South Africa to Freetown, Sierra Leone. To preserve fuel we were steaming slowly at twelve knots using a single boiler and engine. We couldn't do any maneuvering so it was boring. Much of the time we had been in the horse latitudes south of the equator often in the windless doldrums where the sea was so calm that flying fish bouncing along beside us provided almost as much foam as our ship. Richard Rodgers' theme "Beneath the Southern Cross" took on special meaning for me as we made that transit.

We had been at sea so long that our potatoes had turned black with sea water contamination and our flour became infected with weevils. In the film adaptation of Patrick O'Brien's multi-volume nineteenth sea saga, "Master and Commander," Captain Jack Aubrey gives a lesson on knocking the weevils out of a roll. I recognized the technique. So to alleviate our tedium in the twentieth century, our Captain drew on an old Royal Navy tradition and scheduled an old-fashioned Rope Yarn Sunday of games and silliness.

Like a small town's Independence Day celebration, we held three-legged races, tugs of war, and water fights. Stopping the engine, we rigged a climbing net on the hull's side. We were invited to walk the plank and plunge into the sea. To provide protection from possible sharks, several riflemen were stationed aloft – not a reassuring gesture. Nonetheless, I and a small number of shipmates jumped in. Now diving into waves and riding them into the beach is great fun.

But it was scary jumping into a glassy sea. Scariest was the uncertainty of what was below you in the abyss. And the thought that there is probably NOTHING for a mile or so is even more frightening.

Into the Red Sea

11. ON ASBESTOS AND CABIN MATES

My stateroom on the Cotten was in officer's country below decks forward on the port side. To avoid being tossed out of the sack in heavy weather, I slept with my back braced against the exterior bulkhead. The ship's steel skin was so thin and battered by twelve years of steaming that I could hear and feel the rushing sea just inches away. It was quite comforting and provided some of my best sleeping ever.

Less comforting, however, have been the warnings that emerged in later years about the dangers of shipboard asbestos. To provide temperature and sound insulation, virtually every surface was covered with the dangerous mineral. I slept for over 1000 nights (and some days) with my nose less than twelve inches from the painted insulation. It didn't appear to be friable so, so far no problem (knock on wood).

My cabin mate for eighteen months was my boss, the Gunnery Officer. Lieutenant John Lee was a senior

USS Cotten Logo

full Lieutenant overdue for promotion to Lieutenant Commander. He was also said to be the senior African American commissioned officer in the United States Navy. Lieutenant Lee had been an all-American football player at Indiana University in the 1940's when he volunteered for naval service. He wanted to be a quartermaster-meteorologist. In this pre-military integration era, however, the only enlisted position available to him was as a steward. This was not John's ambition so he investigated his options and found that he could be admitted to Officer Candidate School. Twelve years later he was the Gunnery Officer on the USS Cotten and Senior Watch Officer as well as my cabin mate – and one of the finest men I ever met.

As I have mentioned, I served as Treasurer of the Officers' Mess. This entailed keeping cash in my desk safe. John noted that I was sloppy about locking the safe (I have always found combination locks difficult to operate). He reminded me of the danger of theft. I should have listened. One day I discovered that $100 was missing. I was so embarrassed about my carelessness that I decided not to report the loss to anyone. I made up the deficit from my modest monthly pay – about two weeks' worth.

My successor as Treasurer was less timid. When he discovered a similar theft, he reported it immediately. The Naval Criminal Investigative Service (NCIS) was called in. They determined that an officers' steward had stolen the money; he had been observed counting it in the officer's head. I was interviewed and given a polygraph test so my prior secret came out. I long felt some guilt about creating the theft temptation.

Racial discrimination was still alive in the U.S. Navy where it was a bit stronger and lasted longer than in the other services. When at sea, however, prejudice was less obvious because job performance was the basis for respect. In port, outside attitudes intruded. On our voyage to the Middle East, we put in for fuel and supplies in Simons Town, South Africa. Before landing, the Commodore informed us that the South African authorities were making special arrangements for our black crew members going on liberty. They would be met at the pier and provided exclusive transportation to the segregated areas of Cape Town.

With some embarrassment the Commodore C. spoke to Lt. Lee describing the situation and requesting his cooperation in explaining the unhappy facts to our minority shipmates. Like all military "requests" from a senior officer, it is wise to interpret them as veiled orders. Lee cooperated without complaint, but inside he was seething. As a result he went ashore with his black shipmates and proceeded to get roaring drunk. Now getting drunk on the beach was not forbidden to officers, but doing so with enlisted personnel, especially direct subordinates, was a no-no.

When Lee returned to the ship with his celebrating group (they had been treated royally by the local native population), he had to be helped aboard. It cost him. Like many ambitious minority professionals, he had been put in a double bind: expected to accept differentiated treatment, but still held to inflexible traditional majority rules. For me, John was a marvelous mentor and I was well trained to replace him as Gunnery Officer when he was detached for another assignment.

We departed Simons Town and steamed south, then around the Cape of Good Hope and east into the fabled steep rollers of the Indian Ocean passing to port the most majestic view of shore from any sea – Table Mountain towering over Cape Town.

Table Mountain, Cape Town, South Africa

12. INTO THE RED SEA

In 1957 we patrolled the Red Sea west of Saudi Arabia and east of Ethiopia. It was unceasingly hot - in that pre-air conditioned era, my stateroom temperature rarely went below 100 degrees Fahrenheit. All of us tried to maximize our time on deck, sleeping under the stars topside when possible. We recognized what we were in for when we had rendezvoused in the Persian Gulf with the ship we were replacing – a white hulled tropically outfitted seaplane tender, the USS Valcour (AVP-55).

Why were we in the Middle-East? President Eisenhower had become livid when British, French and Israeli forces had attacked Egyptian forces in the Sinai to preserve the West's control of the Suez Canal. Ike sent a small squadron of four ships to the middle east (two in the Persian Gulf and two to the Red Sea) to "interpose" ourselves between the warring parties. We were to sail north to the Gulf of Aquaba and Sharm el Sheikh near the southern end

Aden (British Crown Colony) in 1957

of the Suez Canal (which by then was clogged with sunken ships). The United States politically and morally seemed to side with the Arab forces and was attempting to dissuade the attackers from continuing. Unhappily, the U.S. had no bases in the area and we were actually dependent on the Royal Navy facilities in the British crown colony of Aden on the southern tip of the Arabian Peninsula. Legend says that Aden was originally the site of the biblical paradise Eden. East of Eden would be more appropriate. It was rocky, hot and dry. More recently, on October 12, 2000, it was the location of a suicide attack on the USS Cole (DDG 67) which killed seventeen sailors.

In spite of our ambiguous position, the British port authorities were cordial in responding to our logistical needs. Our buffeted ship badly needed a repainting when we reached Aden. But we were out of U.S. Navy regulation Battleship Gray so we borrowed some Royal Navy Sea Foam Grey-green paint. Never did a United States warship look better.

Maybe it was our lovely new paint in royal colors that led the Queen's Counsel to invite all the ship's officers to celebrate one of our shipmate's promotion to Lieutenant with a "wetting down party." The selection of alcohol was somewhat limited in this Muslim community so brandy was our primary poison. And it was quite a potent poison. Any past and present American-English tensions were out of our minds in our out of our minds joviality.

In town, however, the Royal Navy and United States Navy enlisted personnel were not so congenial (or they had enjoyed less access to alcohol). We received a frantic call from the local police that our sailors were fighting out on the docks. The British Tars thought that their long term Yankee allies had deserted them. In our own inebriated states, we commissioned officers had to run to the pier to break up the fracas. Never had I previously experienced the brandy induced hangover that plagued me the next day. Our suffering Captain seemed out of it for two days.

USS Cotten in Aden 1957

Shortly thereafter we disentangled ourselves from the British by sailing north into the Red Sea to the Ethiopian port of Massawa in the province of Eritrea. The port had been developed by the Italians after Mussolini's ill-fated invasion in the 1930's. Inland from the shorefront were arid rolling hills of sand, rock and parched scrub – no trees and no shade. One day we borrowed a jeep and went hunting antelope in the hills guided by a young male native who effortlessly ran ahead of us (no wonder the Ethiopians do so well in international long distant races). He could spot the prey a mile away shouting out "Kudu, kudu." In the sun's glare and the shimmering heat, I couldn't see a thing and never got off a shot.

The unofficial mayor of Massawa seemed to be Sophie: the Owner-Manager-Chief Madame of the Trocadero Bar. Like many Ethiopians, she was quite beautiful with a regal bearing. She communicated confidence and competence in meeting her various responsibilities. Sophie's business certainly did well during the Cotten's port visits. One of our junior officers became so enamored of Sophie that we feared for his marriage.

Massawa was an active port with ships from around the world. The Captain thought it would be good international relations if we invited a Japanese freighter to join us in a baseball game. He felt that the crew would enjoy a playful break. As I was the Cotten's designated Recreation Officer, the Captain suggested that I try to find some beer to enliven the game. Finding the beer in the Middle East was not easy, but I did purchase 100 cases of Philippine San Miguel lager. Finding the ice to cool the beer was even harder, but all came together and we played ball on a field within sight of the ship.

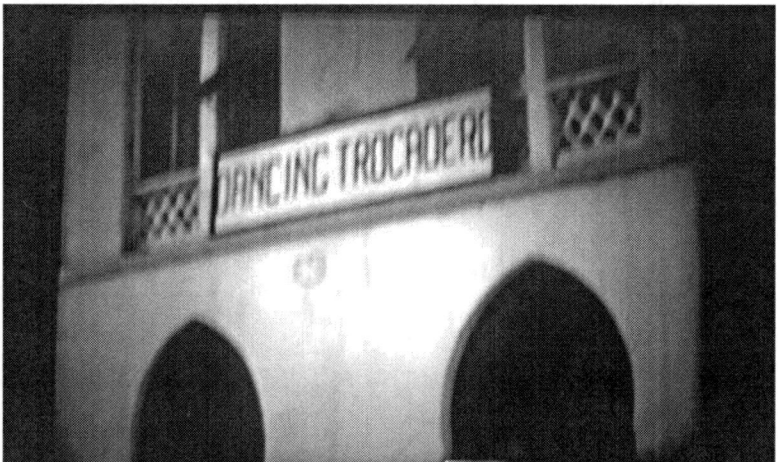

The Trocadero Nightclub in Massawa 1957

And it was a glorious sight with the American Navy sailors and the Japanese merchantmen engaging in their joint national pastimes. Around the fifth inning the Captain warned me not to allow all the beer to be consumed. He thought thirty cases would be sufficient. Since some 200 sailors were partying, this would be approximately three cans per person. In an act of wise circumspection I nodded and did not disclose that we were already up to sixty cases.

Luckily, Captain Bachhuber never discovered my dissembling. My next initiative as Recreation Officer was a tamer bingo night. It was an artistic success, but not so financially. I lost $13.

Into the Red Sea

13. ILLNESS AT SEA

Virtually everyone suffers from some motion sickness on a destroyer. These small, narrow beamed ships bounce around a lot. Most sailors require a few days to reacclimatize to the sea after a few weeks in port. I was no exception. Indeed, I discovered that as the years passed and I rose up the ladder to more responsible positions, my susceptibility to being sick increased. Higher positions brought more deskwork below decks in confined spaces which increased my queasiness.

Being seriously ill on a small combatant is a major problem. Two days out from Trinidad on a cross-Atlantic voyage, a senior Petty Officer had an attack of appendicitis. All we could do was pack him in ice and return to Port of Spain to drop him off. Our Chief Engineer had to be left in Cape Town when he also had appendicitis pain. The presence of a physician is very rare. Larger battleships and aircraft carriers will carry a medical and dental staff, but not a ship with less than three hundred crew members. So it was with much pain that I dealt with two major dental problems during my time at sea. The first was an impacted wisdom tooth. The pain was greater than I had ever experienced before.

By chance, at the time we were carrying a young obstetrician (don't ask why he was assigned to an all-male warship). However, he knew little about easing dental pain. When the pain pills that he prescribed made me too unstable to stand my watches, he tried injecting Novocain into the appropriate facial nerve. Unhappily, he couldn't find the nerve and I couldn't stand the jabs.

The Captain finally concluded that a drugged Ensign Webber was of no use to the ship so he radioed the task force Commodore. A decision was made to helicopter me to the carrier we were screening. That was exciting. The copter hovered over the bouncing fantail; I threw a ring over my head and under my arms and we lifted off. I hadn't expected the aircraft to fly away before I was lifted aboard, so I dangled twenty feet above the water as it began flying to the carrier. Alas, the trip was in vain. The dentist said my tooth was infected and he couldn't operate until the infection was eliminated. A massive dose of penicillin was given and back to the Cotten I was ferried. As

Helicopter approaching the USS Cotten fantail

my feet touched down on the fantail, the Captain broadcast over the ship's loudspeaker: "Ensign Webber report to the bridge for duty." Thankfully, he was joking.

Unhappily, I was extremely allergic to the antibiotic. Patches of my skin began to peel off. My ward room colleagues soon were joking that their evening entertainment was to watch "Ross's skin fall off." In time, the infection lifted and I survived thus saving the Navy the cost of removing my wisdom teeth by waiting until I was released from active duty.

But the Navy was not finished with my mouth. About a year later I came down with a disorder that in World War I had been termed "trench mouth". The modern name was Vincent's infection after the bacterial agent. I was told it was quite common among young naval officers because of job stress (and poor oral hygiene). Uncomfortable as it was, however, it was not debilitating and I could stand my watches. I just couldn't eat. The years of periodontal work came later.

My problems, however were trivial compared to our Supply Officer Ltjg Howard Stern who came down with acute appendicitis while we were in the Red Sea, We were alone on detached duty so no other ship was accompanying us. The nearest medical facilities were in the adjacent Arab countries. But our supply officer was Jewish and they refused to grant him

Preparing patient for evacuation

entry. With great trepidation, our fledgling OB-Gyn Doc prepared the ward room dining table for an emergency operation. Luckily, a Navy PBM Mariner seaplane was able to reach us and ferry the ailing patient to a friendlier site.

This unhappy incident certainly brought home to me the inhumanity of ideological/religious/political divisions.

14. A CATHOLIC CHAPLAIN?

The Cotten didn't have permanent space for a chaplain. However, for a short time we did have a visiting Roman Catholic priest aboard as a Navy chaplain. He roomed in my cabin and we became friendly. He soon became quite unhappy, however, because of disagreements with the Executive Officer. The XO refused to allow the Chaplain to say prayers and give blessings over the public address system because he didn't want to expose the crew as a "captive audience" to Catholic prayers. The priest had not experienced this before. To his relief I'm sure, he was shortly transferred to another destroyer.

When without a Chaplain and at sea for an extended period, the Navy encouraged the Captain to arrange services for the various religious groups represented on board. By ironic chance, at twenty-three years of age, I was the senior Roman Catholic aboard. It fell to me to invite my co-religionists to a

Transferring the Chaplain to USS Daly (DD 519)

prayer service on Sundays. The irony was that until a short three years before I had been an Episcopalian for it was the church into which I was baptized and confirmed. To be sure, my background was fairly high church so my conversion didn't involve a big liturgical jump.

Fortunately, a senior and wise First Class Bosn's Mate of French Canadian extraction was of great help as we arranged services following the Roman Missal's calendar. I have no idea what proportion of the ship's 250 sailor compliment was R.C., but we usually had a group of twenty or so assembled on the torpedo deck if the weather was good. We would say the Rosary and I especially enjoyed reading from the 46th Psalm:

God is our refuge and strength, a very present help in trouble.

Therefore will not we fear, though the earth be removed, and though the mountains be carried into the midst of the sea;

Though the waters thereof roar and be troubled, though the mountains shake with the swelling thereof.....

He maketh wars to cease unto the end of the earth; he breaketh the bow, and cutteth the spear in sunder; he burneth the chariot in fire.

In a world not supportive of an open display of faith, it took some courage for our young seamen visibly to identify themselves as Catholics by attending. I doubt that even I would have participated if the Captain had not made his expectation so clear.

A psychologist might observe that I resolved my uncertainty about appearing as a Catholic by becoming even more committed and she would be right. Play acting can strengthen the real thing. The teenage sailors in my group at least got to see that a presumably intelligent Princeton graduate privileged officer acted on his faith as many of their parents did.

On April 13, 1957 I wrote to Mary Lou: "I've just come from rosary. We say it most evenings around 1900. Usually, there are about fifteen white hats and myself. It seems a long time since we were together at bed time when you would be kneeling saying your prayers and I would be across the bed touching your hands and saying mine. I may be a poor Catholic, but I am certainly glad that I am one."

15. BREAKING RULES

Violating some protocol and regulations is sometimes an operational necessity. Indeed violating some rules seems to increase a leader's prestige in the eyes of the crew. The charismatic Commanding Officer who violates the guidelines for ship handling is granted by his followers additional power beyond a Captain's legitimate authority. Rather than inching his vessel into the pier or incrementally pulling alongside an oil tanker for refueling, the risk oriented Captain will come in engines all full and quickly order all back or stop at just the right propitious moment thus dramatically signaling his arrival.

Such maneuvers are not recommended for even a Boston Whaler, but they did draw oohs and aahs from young sailors. It was especially exciting when refueling from a battleship whose band would be playing with the music bouncing and sea spray churning between our hulls.

Refueling from the USS Wisconsin (BB-64)

Perhaps the most admired by the young men was the Captain who granted more generous liberty or leave than was customary. This creation of upward flowing authority is understandable considering their ages and circumstances of most of the crew. Many had just left home or escaped from authoritarian parents. To serve under a charismatic commander who shared their skepticism about authority and rules was quite motivating.

Of course to be such a commander can be career risking – especially in peace time when there is less opportunity to demonstrate dramatic victories on the other side of the ledger. Sometimes the incoming ship ends up on the beach rather than alongside the pier. Or the high lines and oil lines at sea are ruptured by the surges from a speed differential between the two ships.

Unhappily, I was a close observer of such a surge that severely injured one of my deck hands. In setting up a refueling or transfer at sea, the two ships have to maintain identical course and speed thus keeping a constant distance between the ships. This can be difficult for a small combatant alongside a large one like a battleship. At a critical moment, a seaman standing atop our number two turret was disconnecting the light bolo line in order to hook on a much stronger one. There was a precise moment when the sailor's hand was in the bight (loop) of the line. At that instant the two ships surged apart. The line snapped tight catching the seaman's hand and pilling off most of his fingers and hand skin.

The helmsman who was just at eyelevel with the unfortunate sailor fainted at the sight while the

Officer of the Deck frantically tried to reduce the distance between the ships to lessen the line's tension. At this critical juncture, to my surprise, one of my least reliable and most troublesome seamen jumped up on the turret with his open knife to cut the bleeding man free. Solders in battle have often commented that some of the most courageous acts are committed by unexpected colleagues.

Taking on ammunition is the most important activity at which scrupulous adherence to rules is paramount. Most depots are isolated to minimize collateral damage should an accident occur. For Newport based ships, the ammunition depot was on Prudence Island in Narragansett Bay. However, we did once take on ammunition at sea from an Ammunition ship (AE). Watching 5 inch 38 caliber shells coming across in a canvas harness just a few feet above the surging water separating the two ships was an awesome sight. The most dangerous moment, however, was unhooking the cradles as the deck was surging below one's feet.

Thankfully, we didn't drop any.

16. TO DRINK OR NOT TO DRINK

Since boyhood I have been a naval history buff, I would pore over accounts of sea battles: The Dutch Admiral de Ruyter defeating the British at the raid at the River Medway in 1667; the Japanese Admiral Togo devastating the Russian fleet in the Tsushima Strait in 1905; And sadly, another Japanese Admiral Mikawa defeating the sunset lighted U.S. Navy at Savo Island in 1942. So it was with special delight in November 1958 when the Cotten put into Portsmouth, England where Lord Nelson's flagship *Victory* is frozen in sand and time. Even coming from a modern American warship, the *Victory* is an impressive sight. It's freeboard (hull height above the waterline) is so much greater than a destroyers. And while we had four main battery guns, the *Victory* carried a hundred.

To stand on the deck where Nelson gave his famous commands and to see where he received his mortal wound was a moving experience for me. Of course it was childish romanticism on my part, but I stand by it. Immaturity has driven some men and women to great deeds in behalf of family, faith and nation. Now fifty years later with the supposed wisdom of age, I recognize so much of war and heroism is jingoistic nonsense. Nonetheless, I still fondly remember my visit to the *Victory* and the history it evoked.

Unlike on Nelson's flagship and Royal Navy ships ever since, the United States Navy has no tradition of a

HMS Victory, Portsmouth, United Kingdom

daily grog ration for the crew or an officer's ward room bar. Like many American institutions, the U.S. Navy is ambivalent about alcoholic beverages. Regulations ban alcoholic beverages from being stocked or served onboard ships.

This difference was especially clear to me when in October 1958 I was detailed to a Halifax based Canadian Corvette for joint Atlantic exercises. At their appointed afternoon hour, the Canadian ward room had an open bar with all kinds of beverages available. It was certainly used (and I joined in), but I never observed excessive consumption. The social mores kept drinking under control; the cost for breaking the code was just too great to risk it.

The American prohibition onboard lies deep in our history of religious injunctions, strong individuality, and weak social controls. The U.S. Navy fears that drinking on board would be uncontrollable, undermining teamwork and a ship's readiness for combat. The partying of our officers and sailors when on liberty doesn't lend support for relaxing the shipboard alcohol prohibition.

The alternation of long dry periods at sea with periodic port visits seems to encourage maximum consumption when available. Indeed, some outright alcoholics were able to be valuable shipmates because of the shipboard forced sobriety (except for the first couple of days after leaving port while they are recovering). The brightest officer colleague that I ever had was a problem drinker. Once, on departing from Naples, we had already cast off all lines when Lieutenant F. appeared running down the pier leaping the widening water gap. We were pleased to have his communications skill back on board, but he spent the first twenty four hours in his rack. The Executive Officer was livid when he couldn't awaken him for duty.

I violated regulations just once. When we were in the Red Sea, I was the ship's Torpedo Officer as well as an auxiliary assignment as the ship's Recreation Officer. This is a dangerous combination. Our torpedoes were fueled by the purest two hundred proof unadulterated alcohols known to man. And I had the only keys to the storage locker.

On one occasion my torpedo gang was unable to enjoy any shore liberty in Massawa because they were preparing our torpedoes for possible action upon our Monday departure. They worked all day in a broiling tropical sun. To reward them I broke out a limited supply of alcohol which when mixed with canned grape juice makes a drinkable if potent confection. For a time, morale soared – another example, albeit a dangerous one, of how rule violation can build greater willingness to follow a leader.

Fortunately, our torpedo shoot on March 12, 1957 went perfectly. I wrote to Mary Lou that everything was going so well for me that I feared when "this bubble will break."

Into the Red Sea

17. WE RUN OUT OF AFTERSHAVE LOTION

U.S. Navy ships include a small store at which crew can purchase personal necessities like tooth paste and shaving supplies. The stores are expected to be self-supporting. One day the Supply Officer told me that Cotten's store was sold out of aftershave lotion. One of my Chief Petty Officers (CPOs) had been buying bottles by the dozen. I wondered why. Since the alcohol content of the lotion exceeded fifty percent, I suspected that it was not being splashed on a newly shaven face.

The purchaser was a CPO retread – a senior enlisted man who had risen to Chief Boatswain's Mate and then underwent retraining to convert to Chief Electronics Technician. This is the most difficult retooling in military service. The intellectual skills are just so difficult for someone of limited education moving from deck seamanship to electronic concepts. And Chief Ed X had not made a happy transition. His work as an ET was subpar and he was feeling the pressure. I don't know if his drinking problem preceded or followed his transition, but it may have exacerbated the behavior.

A competent ET is one of the most valuable assets to a ship, especially because a small combatant like a destroyer is allotted only one. This incident gave me a reason to seek his transfer from the ship with minimum loss of face. Having a drinking problem is less of a black mark on one's record than unsatisfactory performance. We were able to offer a transfer to a shore facility.

I wasn't proud that I had possibly foisted an inadequate ET onto another command without being candid about his performance. But I was desperate for a replacement. I never received a new Chief ET, but a couple of months later a new officer arrived who was a mustang electronics technician. That is, he was a commissioned officer who had formerly been a First Class Petty Officer Electronics Technician. He had gone to officer candidate school and been commissioned as a Lieutenant Junior Grade.

And he was a crackerjack ET - so much so that in extremis I had him focus on his expert skills rather than his officer responsibilities. Our single most sophisticated electronics system was called the Target Designation System (TDS). Using multiple radars and console joy sticks, a fire control officer would assign targets to the five inch and three inch antiaircraft guns. Without the system, coordinating firing at multiple enemy aircraft would be impossible. It would be a dangerous free for all.

When the system malfunctioned, our mission performance capability was severely compromised (up there with losing our Sonar). When we had a breakdown that was beyond the capability of our second class ET to fix, I directed Lt. Y to focus exclusively on fixing the equipment until it was repaired. This was clearly beyond my authority and it couldn't be enforced if he objected to the truncation of his duties. After all, he had advanced from specialist enlisted duties to the higher status of commissioned line officer. Fortunately for me, he understood the seriousness of the situation and agreed. After several days he was able to virtually rebuild the system and restore us to operational readiness.

And he didn't buy excessive aftershave.

Into the Red Sea

18. THE MEANING OF LIBERTY

The Navy assumes that enlisted men belong to the service twenty four hours a day, seven days a week. "Liberty" occurs when a sailor is allowed to leave the ship or post for a limited number of hours. The traditional increments are: (a) overnight until 0600 in the morning, (b) thirty six hours (usually Saturday noon until Monday morning), (c) forty eight hours (usually Friday afternoon until Monday morning), and (d) seventy two hours − a rare goody over a holiday weekend. Of course all of a ship's crew couldn't be let off at the same time so the crew is usually divided into three sections. At sea the three sections rotate around the clock on four hour watches. In port, at least one section must be on board so weekend leave is much coveted.

When I was on the Iowa, I had received a three day pass to visit London. The ship was anchored in Edinburgh, Scotland where the crew seemed to be receiving a particularly warm welcome from the Scots. I decided to take the train to London. A big mistake. I came down with food poisoning from something eaten enroute and spent all three days sick and in bed in a very modest hotel.

In general, leaving the ship with your liberty section was a given unless some disciplinary action restricted you. To leave one simply showed your precious liberty card. But you had to have a card in your hand – and as a division officer I kept them in my pocket before they were handed out. This control was a flexible means to delay or hold a sailor who had not completed his tasks satisfactorily. Being able to hold or hand out these cards was raw power. However, this practice was subject to arbitrary and prejudicial decisions so it was against Navy regulations. The rule stipulated liberty couldn't be withheld unless a due process proceeding such as a Captain's Mast or Court Martial dictated it.

Understandably, some officers felt that blind adherence to this rule would sharply reduce their disciplinary power – and more importantly, reduce their ability informally to reward exceptional performance with unofficial liberty. Liberty cards were the coin of the realm in the Navy – more precious than money.

US Navy Liberty Boat Piraeus, Greece 1958

Returning from liberty to an anchored ship in small boat loaded with a mix of sober and drunk sailors can be adventurous. In smaller ports, we had to anchor up to several miles out. Our life boats were used as launches holding a couple dozen passengers a trip. The heady mix of youthful passions and local beer often led to misunderstandings and fisticuffs. One of the most challenging such trips occurred when we were anchored off Lisbon, Portugal in 1958.

Navy life boats from the mid-twentieth century were throwbacks to the nineteenth. A helmsman stood tall on the stern platform steering with a tiller while ringing a small bell to signal the mid-boat engine operator to put the engine at half, fall, forward or reverse. Crowding around the two man crew was the mixed bag of passengers.

On this trip, Seaman First Sam K was at the helm. Now, Sam was as handsome a Navy man as one could imagine - right out of central casting for a film of Herman Melville's *Billy Budd*. Even I can remember the play of his thigh muscles in his white bellbottoms as he maintained his balance on choppy water while steering the small boat. He was a ballet dancer. Unfortunately, the turmoil on board was threatening to tumble him into the water.

A young Ensign, Bruce Hilyard, and I were returning when one blotto sailor pulled a knife. He tried to attack Sam K to continue some earlier dispute which threatened our boat's stability. To my surprise, the usually quiet Hilyard grabbed the offender in his arms and thrust the sailor's face underwater while I held his legs,   After bobbing along in the water for a while, the angry young sailor soon stopped struggling. Talk about water boarding! I thought we had drowned him. Happily the water soaked sailor either came to his senses or entirely lost them because we were able to haul him back aboard and to the brig in a much more subdued state.

That was the only time I saw our small ship's brig utilized as anything other than for locking up the medical corpsman's precious allotment of medicinal spirits.

Into the Red Sea

19. ON SHORE PATROL

When U.S. Navy ships visit a foreign port, a shore patrol unit is organized to assist local police authorities in controlling the behavior of the visiting crews and reducing conflicts with the resident population.   I was appointed to this duty on numerous occasions.

Aden provided one of the strangest of these shore patrol assignments. I was assigned to accompany Royal Air Force Police from the local British base. I soon felt like I was immersed in a replay of the British Raj.   Without any weapons, but with apparent confidence in their racial and moral superiority, the Brits would walk into a local tavern while Ramadan was being celebrated and haul out whomever they suspected as being potential troublemakers. Nervously following along with my 45 caliber sidearm and Billy club, I thought I might be assaulted any moment by the angry natives.

But fear can be a powerful deterrent. During my Aden service British World War II era Lancaster bombers flew over some neighboring mud villages and dropped leaflets that demanded the handover of some suspected terrorists and threatened a bombing for noncompliance.   Thinking back over the years, it is sort of nostalgic to remember an era when the British, not the Americans, were the most disliked people in the world.

Royal Air Force Avro Lancaster

In Santiago de Cuba my responsibilities required me to tour five "clubs" (houses of prostitution). The attitude of the U.S. Navy at the time reflected realistic hypocrisy. We wanted the sailors to have rest and relaxation (R&R), to mingle with the foreign locals, pursue good international relations, and show the flag. Expected was that the R and R for our mainly 18-23 year old crew would involve some steamy sex.

With a couple of my Petty Officers all of us clad in immaculate whites, 45's and billy clubs, we would patrol the whore houses mainly trying to sort out payment disputes and control the fights over football team rivalries, inter-ship disputes, and territorial claims to the most attractive women.

Striding with feigned confidence into the house bars, I would be greeted playfully by the resident ladies. They wanted to feel my billy club and asked how big was my gun. Offers to sample their wares were proffered which they knew couldn't be accepted because of my duty status. I wrote to Mary Lou that one bar girl in Massawa tried to climb on my shoulders. Amidst all the joking, I came to feel that they genuinely trusted us to protect them from out of control sailors. Alas, some of visits were less enjoyable. A shattered beer bottle thrust into the face of a fighting sailor can inflict serious injury (not to mention the difficulty of cleaning the blood stains out of my precious whites).

111

The worst shore patrol experience occurred in May 1957 in Mombasa, Kenya. Liberty hours were expiring and I was waiting at the pier for late stragglers. Several arrived in a taxi and began arguing loudly with the driver over what they considered an exorbitant fare.   Language misunderstandings and extortion attempts made this a common dispute.   In short order local police became involved, not surprisingly taking the driver's side.

Not wanting the incident to escalate into an international affair, I ordered the sailors to double what they thought appropriate (which was about half of what the driver demanded). I then gathered about a dozen men in a group and began marching toward our liberty boat to return to the ship. The Kenyan police ordered us to stop so they could arrest the offending sailors.   I had to make a decision. What I did still surprises me with its hint of assumed cultural superiority.   I ordered the sailors to keep walking. I was not going to allow three of our company to be imprisoned in an African jail.   The police then drew their guns issuing threats in a language I couldn't understand.   I guess I just assumed that they would not risk the ire of the United States Government by firing. And they didn't.

Afterwards, I felt much like the Ugly American of international notoriety.

Into the Red Sea

20. THE HOTTEST AND COLDEST PLACES

To send a Cold War message to the Soviet Union, in September 1957 a NATO task force was dispatched from Halifax, Nova Scotia for winter maneuvers in the North Sea between Iceland and Norway. On the way we anchored for a short time in Scapa Flow the northern wartime base of the Royal Navy in World War One. On May 30, 1916 the fleet had steamed out to fight the German Navy off of Jutland in history's largest naval battle. As we cruised by Jutland, I could almost feel the ghosts of the 8,500 sailors who had died there.

The NATO mission task was to intimidate the Soviets by showing that we could operate in the worst of climate and sea conditions. And it was the worst. Ice formed on all of our exposed surfaces. Touching metal ran a risk of leaving patches of skin behind. Green sea water would break over the bow rolling down the decks and icing up the safety lines, decks and gun barrels. The coating became so thick that we began to fear for the ship's stability as topside weight accumulated. Our painting chipping hammers were utilized to remove what ice we could. Strange but in the midst of all this ice, officers continued to wear their dress leather soled shoes. We had no others.

Like most behavior pertaining to things military, these foolhardy exercises produced conflicting attitudes: pride that we did what we did to show the Russians and sorrow for the planes and pilots lost in crashes. I still treasure my Blue Nose Certificate for service beyond the Arctic Circle. It is right next to my Shellback Certificate for sailing south of the equator into the earth's hottest zones.

The cruise back the States provided an especially satisfying experience. I taught a mathematics course to our senior petty officers thus learning the truism that teaching provides the best learning. And using old fashioned star sights and sun lines I navigated the ship to Point Judith and then to Fall River, Massachusetts. This was before satellites and the GPS so I became intimate with my sextant and favorite stars, Sirius, Vega, and Betelgeuse. We arrived on time within yards of our destination.

Waiting on the tender USS Yosemite (AD19) upon our arrival on a cold December day was my wife and our new three month old daughter Sarah whom I then met for the first time.

There were more hot zones than cold ones, a reflection of the location of spots troublesome to the United States. Cuba and Puerto Rico were certainly warm as were the Persian Gulf and the Red Sea. A summer day in Piraeus, Greece was no picnic. The salt flats outside of Massawa, Eritrea were routinely 120 degrees Fahrenheit. I will never forget the giant insects buzzing me in the glare of the sodium lights on the pier in a stifling hot port of Freetown, Sierra Leone. Years later, after examining the skin on my face a dermatologist asked if I had spent a lot of time in the sun!

The absolute hottest for me was in the good old continental U.S. standing in a Midshipman's dress whites on a blacktop parade ground at the Naval Air Station in Corpus Christi, Texas. The shimmering heat waves so distorted my vision that I barely saw colleagues around me collapsing onto the hot pavement.

Marching on the August sands of Little Creek Virginia in Tidewater humidity with a full back pack had been hot, but no one fainted. Perhaps movement saved us. Standing on the asphalt in Texas in August 1955 was too much. When I woke up in the Navy dispensary, a Medical Corpsman was analyzing my blood with an exclamation, "Your blood has consistency of "Jell-O!"

My drinking a dozen Coca-Colas a day (I couldn't stand the local water) was clogging up my arteries with sugar. Years later as an officer I used to store cases of Coke in the bottom drawer of my state room chest. It came in especially helpful when the ship sprung a pinhole leak allowing its bunker oil to percolate into our fresh water storage. The Cokes were better than the Jell-O-like bug juice that the mess offered.

It took me twenty five years to break the Coca Cola (classic) habit. Thank you Coke Zero!

21. ON COFFEE AND CANNED HAMS

Travelers to Cape Cod are familiar with the terrible traffic backups and long delays when they try to cross from the mainland to the Cape. The Bourne and Sagamore bridges cross over the seventeen mile long Cape Cod Canal which connects Buzzard's Bay in the south to Cape Cod Bay in the north. On a snowy 1958 Christmas Eve, our ship had the different experience of passing under the bridges enroute from Newport to Boston Naval Shipyard in Charlestown, Massachusetts. I assume the holiday timing was to minimize encountering any other vessels. It was certainly resented by the crew. Nonetheless, it was a beautiful trip.

The canal is quite narrow so even a small combatant like our destroyer seemed huge in barely clearing the bridges. The mainland side was especially close with Christmas lights sparkling on every building. A light snow was falling. It was almost festive. We sailed to the shipyard for a two month maintenance overhaul that was scheduled every couple of years. Worn equipment and machinery would be repaired or

Cape Cod Canal and Bourne Bridge

replaced. Upgrades in electronics and weapons would be installed.

Although the budget was limited and planning extensive, there was surprising flexibility in actual projects completed. Unauthorized modifications might be accomplished with appropriate encouragement of yard personnel. The informal medium of exchange was not money, but coffee, hams, and cigarettes (and a bottle now and then of whiskey). The trade was truly impressive.

Exchanging ship's surplus supplies for unofficial yard work enabled a ship's crew to upgrade their living spaces and general quality of shipboard life. My second division was delighted to obtain linoleum titles which they laid to cover the dingy grey painted steel deck in their sleeping space. The bright green and white did cheer them up. Unfortunately, there are risks in such unauthorized "improvements." They add weight that increases the vessel's displacement of water so that it sinks deeper into the water thus increasing resistance and reducing speed. And weight above the ship's waterline affects stability and increases a risk of capsizing in extreme weather.

Nonetheless, even the Captain got into the game using yard carpenters to construct a replica sailing ship's main mast inside the officers ward room. The "mast" did not extend through the overhead (ceiling) and it had no operational function. Its lovely oak sheathing seemed merely to feed the CO's illusion that he was commanding a Naval sailing frigate of the 1770's vintage. Silly of course, but romantic boyhood images can be motivating for a peacetime sailor wishing for military excitement in harm's way.

22. "FAMILIAL" TIES

Becoming an effective naval officer requires trusting your senior Petty Officers, respecting their skills, and accepting becoming dependent on them. They of course are dependent on you. This interdependence could extend off the ship into private lives. At age twenty four, a young commissioned officer can find himself as a surrogate parent or older brother to a nineteen year old sailor who has messed up his life on the beach.

One of my young charges was arrested in Fall River, Massachusetts and charged with adultery — then a crime in Lizzie Borden's home town. He had picked up an attractive (at least to him at the time in his impaired state) young woman in a bar and she had extended an invitation for him to come to her apartment. And he did. Unfortunately, the rent on the small place was being paid by the woman's husband, a fisherman then out to sea. It was not clear to me who had initiated the charges, but I found myself in the city court serving as a character witness and to pay bail if possible.

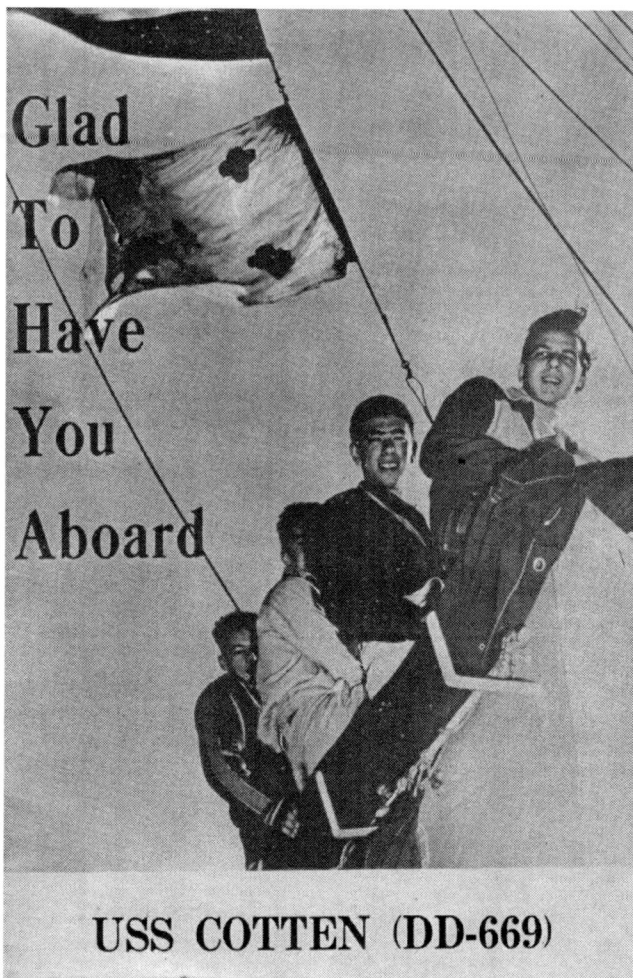

Family Day brochure 1958

Serving in a seafaring town, the Judge understood the youthful frustrations involved so a pragmatic solution to the situation was arranged. I paid the bail and accepted personal custody of the sailor promising his delivery back to the ship in Rhode Island and to see that he didn't return to Fall River.

At the other extreme was a divorce action involving my senior Fire Control technician - a First Class Petty Officer of a well traveled forty years of age. However admirable and valuable a shipmate when at sea, Fred S. had his in-port problems when on liberty or leave. I once had to arrange for the Naval Hospital to fix him up with a new set of teeth because in a drunken stupor he had vomited them into the ship's toilet (which was continuously flushing). They had disappeared into Narragansett Bay.

His wife had apparently run out of patience with his misadventures so he asked me to speak to her and plead his case for reconciliation. At age twenty four I had been married for all of two years so this was a novel request. Apparently I had developed a reputation among the crew as being a particularly straight arrow who successfully eluded the temptations of myriad ports which we had visited.

And they were much impressed with my wife based on her visits for dinner in the ward room when I had Sunday duty. Fred thought this might convey credibility to his wife.

I spoke to the suffering woman with all the wisdom of my advanced years and matrimonial experience. I don't think I had much of an impact because we went back to sea shortly thereafter and the no change in Fred's behavior was evident. But the events certainly reinforced my resolution never to be involved personally in adultery, divorce or vomited dentures!

23. "I HAVE THE CONN"

When a warship is underway, unless the Captain is on the bridge personally directing the ship, the Officer of the Deck (OOD) has responsibility for ordering the ship's course and speed. It is an awesome responsibility. It directly involves the safety of hundreds of fellow crew members. One of the riskiest situations is when a destroyer is screening a carrier task force to protect it from enemy submarines. When the carrier is launching or landing aircraft, it needs to turn into the wind. If the screening vessel misinterprets a "Rum" or "Coke" signal and turns in the wrong direction, a dangerous risk of collision is created. The USS Hobson (DD-464) had been cut in two on April 26, 1952 by the aircraft carrier USS Wasp (CV-18) when the smaller ship's OOD ordered a wrong turn and crossed the larger ship's bow (176 sailors died). On June 3, 1969 74 sailors were lost in a similar collision when the USS Frank E. Evans (DD-754) was cut in two by the Australian carrier HMAS Melbourne.

One of the most satisfying complements in my life was given by a veteran Signals Petty Officer who told me that I was the only OOD that the men had enough confidence in to sleep below decks when we were screening a carrier. Otherwise, they slept on deck closer to the life boats. I suspect the Signalman was exaggerating, but it was flattering.

Plane guarding for the USS Coral Sea (CV 43)

The conning responsibility can become murky when entering an unfamiliar port. Using a local pilot is usually mandatory. He or she joins the Captain and OOD on the bridge and is given temporary control over the ship's movements. But the ship's officers are not totally relieved of their responsibilities. The Cotten once went aground when entering the harbor in Miami, Florida. It had looked easy on the chart, but a shifting sand bar caught us. Luckily, the tide was waxing and after a few minutes we lifted off without blemish to the Captain's record.

A tragic demonstration of command ambiguity occurred when I was bringing the ship into Boston Harbor after a day's sea trials of shipyard repairs. The pilot had assumed the conn watched over by the Captain and me. We were advancing at dead slow speed. Suddenly we heard the dreaded cry of "man overboard." One of the civilian yard workers on board had fallen over the side. Unhappily, the Captain chose to leave the bridge to investigate. Almost simultaneously, a freighter forward of our port bow blew his whistle three times announcing that she was backing out of her slip.

Author as Officer of the Deck 1958

When at sea there is a normal routine to follow in the case of man overboard. One orders the helm over toward the side of the fallen person in order to swing the propellers away. Then one orders all engines to stop. Unhappily, in a crowded Boston Harbor without the immediate presence of the Captain on the bridge and a possible collision with the backing ship ahead, I could not execute the standard maneuver. Instead, Iordered an engine change from slow ahead to all back full. Such a change churned up much watery froth and ran the risk of backing over the fallen worker. But it avoided a potential collision.

Fortunately (for my conscience anyway), recovery and autopsy of the now dead man's body indicated that he had died of a heart attack before he hit the water.

Into the Red Sea

24. A NEAR BREAKDOWN

The United States Navy is a hierarchical organization. Orders generally flow downward with limited consultation. Nonetheless, there is one area where the enlisted personnel have absolute authority – the choice of music to be played over the public address system when the ship is on holiday routine. I shutter to think of the rap that must predominate today, but back in the 1950's it was mainly jazz, swing, Connie Francis, and Frank Sinatra. Nonetheless, the most amazing popularity for any record began when we were in Naples, Italy in 1958. A sailor on shore had heard the song *Volare* by Domenico Madugho and brought the record aboard. The crew was absolutely mesmerized and it was played endlessly. It was a popular hit world wide of course, but it seemed to have special meaning to our young men with its appeal to "flying away into the blue" which many on board wanted to do. Luckily, I had only one personal flight episode.

Success in hierarchical organizations is a mix of merit, politics and luck. All played a role in my climb to third in command as first the Gunnery Officer and later Operations Officer, Navigator, and Senior Watch Officer on the Cotten. When in May 1957 our Gunnery Officer was promoted to Lieutenant Commander, he requested relief so that he could assume a higher post elsewhere. Our Captain asked for a replacement who was a graduate of the Newport Gunnery School, but the Bureau of Personnel in Washington, DC replied that none was available so, "Black as it seems, Ensign Webber will have to be fleeted up to Gunnery Officer." Yes, that was in an official Navy dispatch!

I was a bit frightened, but pleased that it would eventually guarantee a six week assignment at the school in Rhode Island if we ever got there. On that May 19, 1957 day, however, we crossed the equator east of Africa for the fourth time.

My promotion to Operations Officer was similarly fortuitous (at least for me if not my predecessor). The Ops Officer is normally assigned as the general quarters officer of the deck on the bridge with the ship's conn as his battle station. Unfortunately (for him) my predecessor Lieutenant Z. had a hearing problem and was unable to distinguish among the three radio nets that one had to monitor on the bridge. One had to be able to distinguish from which

134

loud speaker a voice was coming and how to respond. It was all babble to my then boss. But it was easy for me and so I was jumped to fill his shoes at GQ and I loved it.

Each ship has a distinct radio call sign. For the Cotten it was "Scarf." Amidst the crackling sounds of three or more radio nets on the bridge, one had to be able to hear your own call sign and recognize who was calling, as in "Scarf, this is Cowboy." The call names became ingrained and never forgotten. Twenty-five years later I received a telephone call from an executive recruiter who greeted me with "Scarf, this is Dancing Girl." He had read my resume, saw I had served in Destroyer Squadron Thirty and assumed that I would recognize his former ship's call sign. Unfortunately, I didn't – perhaps that's why I didn't get an offer for the position for which he was recruiting.

I was formally appointed Operations Officer in 1958 in time for a deployment off of Lebanon that involved a three hundred page ops manual that I had essentially memorized. Literally no one else on board knew more about the details of the task force plans. Shortly thereafter the Navigator, an Annapolis graduate who was a senior lieutenant, had to leave because of an illness so I was also given his responsibilities.

All of this was heady stuff and I performed well receiving a second letter of commendation. But I didn't recognize how stressful it was until maneuvers were completed and the ship returned to our French Riviera port of Beaulieu-sur-Mer. Naturally, we were all anxious to leave the ship and get some drinks. But when ashore in Nice on a lovely veranda overlooking a sparkling sea, I panicked. I simply couldn't face the contrast with the recent past. Perhaps I was faced with too many choices on the beach in an environment that was less structured than life at sea.

I hastily excused myself from the group and proceeded to walk back to the ship. It was at least ten kilometers. But I had to keep moving. I remember that the sole of my right shoe came loose, flapping for miles as I paced.

I didn't leave the ship again during our ten days in port. No one seemed to notice that I was experiencing particular difficulty. As a bonus, however, I was available to assume on board duties for several bachelor officers thus piling up favors to be reciprocated when we returned to Rhode Island

and to my wife and new daughter. One even offered me my liberty days in Nice for his later days in Newport at a one to two ratio. I took the offer and never had another anxiety attack.

We then proceeded to Naples where I assisted in piloting the ship into the Bay with the sun rising above Mount Vesuvius giving me personal connection to the old Italian saying, "See Naples and die." On April 3, 1959 I wrote: "It was a long night as we sighted lights around 0300 and didn't moor until 1100. I had to be on the bridge navigating the whole time. The harbor was fantastically crowded and mooring was very difficult."

From Naples I was able to travel to Rome and be present with 60,000 others cheering "viva Papa" in St. Peter's Basilica on April 11 when Pope John XXIII celebrated a canonization Mass. Big stuff for a twenty three year old convert to Roman Catholicism. I wrote: "The bus trip, hotel room, eight meals and Rome tours cost $26. I only spent $34 in all. I couldn't afford it, but it was an opportunity not to be missed." How times have changed!

Twenty years later I returned to the Riviera with my family to visit the places that I had not seen earlier (well, not quite the same places I would imagine). Gazing down on the empty harbor at Beaulieu-sur-Mer, I could almost see the phantom ship that had been my home and refuge in a time of stress.

USS Cotten in Beaulieu Sur Mere, France 1959

25. A STORM IN RHODES

Weighing anchor and setting to open sea when a storm approaches had been a familiar experience during Narragansett Bay nor'easters. Destroyers with their narrow beams are particularly vulnerable in heavy winds and seas. More World War Two DD's were lost to Pacific typhoons in 1944 and 1945 than were lost in battle. One December in 1958 we sailed into a brutal storm for two days, taking the heavy waves a few points off the port bow. But we were getting so battered that the squadron Commodore decided to reverse course so we could go with the wind and sea taking them on our port quarter (the rear of the hull on the left side).

Turning was dangerous because for a few seconds the waves would be striking our beam with at least some risk of capsizing. On the bridge we watched the incline meter with trepidation as the ship approached the limit of its stability.   The ship righted herself, but running with the waves entailed a terrible corkscrew-like yawing and wallowing that was truly sickening. Seasickness was rampant.

White water over the bow

Our squadron flagship lost its lifeboats and helicopter overboard. We had life boat and substantial superstructure damage. Rivets that attached the aluminum structure to the hull steel turned to powder. Many people suffered cuts and bruises, but no one was lost overboard. What I remember most though is the incredible fatigue generated by the continuous bracing of muscles day after day as the ship pitched and rolled. After three days of misery, we sailed out of the storm and were surprised to discover that we were within sight of Bermuda. The

British graciously supplied us with fuel, food and water, but unhappily wouldn't let us come ashore!

The Mediterranean Island of Rhodes, Greece was the location of another severe storm in May 1959 which precipitated my peak Naval command experience. Ironically, it was just a few days before my scheduled departure from the ship. The harbor in which we were anchored was quite small with limited protection from certain Mediterranean winds. We continually worried about dragging our anchor and drifting on the rocks or into another ship.

The Commanding Officer and Executive Officer were both ashore attending a Commodore's conference when the order came to make ready for sea. I was the Command Duty Officer (CDO) and the most senior person board. Usually the CDO's biggest challenge is to select the evening movie to be shown in the ward room by the most junior officer on board. This was a bit more serious. The sudden storm rose so quickly that neither the CO nor the XO seemed able to return to the ship. Conditions were deteriorating so rapidly that it was imperative that the ships put to sea. And so I issued the command.

Entrance to Harbor at Rhodes, Greece 1959

Fortunately, our Chief Engineering Officer was aboard and the critical sea detail already set so we hauled up the anchor. It was scary as hell to feel the ultimate responsibility for the crew's well-being.

Providentially, just as I gave the command "All ahead slow," the Executive Officer managed to climb aboard from a small boat. So my command of a United States Navy warship underway in foreign waters ended after two minutes.

Sic transit Gloria.

Into the Red Sea

26. SECRET COURIER

When I was detached from the Cotten after three years of full and intensive duty, it was a thrill to be piped over the side by the Bos'n as if I were an ersatz Admiral. Holding onto the silver cocktail shaker that was a gift from my ward room colleagues, I was deposited on the pier in Rhodes and told to find my own way home.

With a $12 cash advance from our Supply Officer, Aristotle's Onassis' Olympic Airlines provided the first leg with a DC3 commercial flight to Athens. I found my way to the United States military facility at the airport inquiring about a flight back to the States. They had nothing for me ....unless I was willing to be a diplomatic courier carrying secret papers that would be chained to my body. Having been away from my family for several months, I accepted with alacrity. But I did have a vision of some terrorists sawing off my arm to steal the attaché case.

So handcuffed to the diplomatic pouch, I flew in a venerable PBM twin engine seaplane sitting in a very

Into the Red Sea

US Navy Martin PBM (US Navy photograph)

Uncomfortable canvas jump seat. The engine noise and rattling was unbelievable. But we made it to Tripoli, Libya. I delivered my precious cargo to an intelligence officer who magically possessed a key that released me from my chains.

After a stiff drink at the Wheelus Air Force Base bar, I hunted up farther eastward flights. Luckily, I landed a seat on a posh Air Force Lockheed Constellation that

146

took me via the Azores to Charleston, South Carolina. After the intensity of life on the Cotten, the trip back was like a blissful dream without demands and responsibilities.

From Charleston I took a train north to New York City where I was released from active duty at the place where it had all started seven years before – 90 Church Street.   The Navy offered me a faculty position at the Naval Academy in Annapolis, Maryland if I would sign up for another term of active duty. It was flattering and tempting, but I had a new baby and was anxious to find a civilian job.

Over the years I have reflected on my luck of the draw: sworn in as a Midshipman in July 1952 as the Korean War was winding down and retired from the Ready Reserve as a Lieutenant in 1966 as the Vietnam War was heating up. I did receive a call back to active duty notice during the 1961 Berlin crisis but the authorities eventually decided that my anti-submarine sea experience was not particularly relevant to Berlin.

An old military aphorism borrows from John Milton's poem on his blindness, "They also serve who only stand and wait." Well, for many months I had stood on violently rolling and pitching decks as the ships in which I had served stood ready to do their duty - if necessary, in harm's way. I was proud and content.

As the years have passed, I have become ever prouder of my Navy years. In all of my later challenging positions, nothing exceeded the Navy in intellectual challenge. Learning the technology of one's ship, memorizing the contents of a thick operations manual, and drawing on both to make action decisions on the fly gives an incredible sense of competence, confidence and achievement.

In my years as a university professor teaching students I would often tell them what a benefit there was there was in serving as a military officer. My very first journal article for the American Management Association described how more effective than business was the military's use of a young graduate's ability. The Navy simply gave greater responsibility more quickly. The students' blank stares and silence would suggest that they either thought my comments were obsolete or that I was nuts. At my undergraduate college this year, only two students were commissioned as officers. In my graduation year we were over two hundred.

Yes, in our era we faced selective service and the military draft for which most of us were eligible. And the United States in 1956 was not involved in any

NROTC Officer Commissioning, Princeton University 1956

wars.   So it was not heroism that prompted our generation to serve. For many, it was simply a belief that becoming an adult in this blessed land meant accepting the responsibility to defend it and to prove one's ability to accept the challenge.

Index

Into the Red Sea

About the Author

Ross Webber was born in New Rochelle, New York. He holds a BS in Engineering from Princeton University, a PhD in Economics from Columbia University, and a honorary MS from the University of Pennsylvania. He served as a Midshipman, Ensign, Lieutenant Junior Grade, and Lieutenant in the United States Navy. He worked as an industrial engineer at the Eastman Kodak Company before joining the faculty of the Wharton School at the University of Pennsylvania. At Penn he served as a Professor of Management, Chairperson of the Management Department, and Vice President for Development and University Relations. He is now Professor Emeritus.

Webber was very active in business and management consulting including serving as a Director and Executive Committee member of The American Water Works Company as well as a Director and Vice Chairman of the Supervisory Board of Arcadis NV, an international engineering firm. He is the author of ten other text and trade books including: BECOMING A COURAGEOUS MANAGER (1991) and THE DOG ATE MY BUDGET: TALES ABOUT TEACHING AND MANAGING IN THE IVY TOWER (2008). He lives in Haddonfield, New Jersey with his wife Mary Louise. They have five children and eighteen grandchildren.

Into the Red Sea

CPSIA information can be obtained at www.ICGtesting.com
Printed in the USA
LVOW081019130712

289941LV00005B/5/P

9 781460 920954